KOKEY KOALA
and the
Bush Olympics

Poem and concept by **Trixie Whitmore**
Illustrations by **Claire Yerbury** & **Marlene Nash**

murray david publishing

Can you find the  Copperhead Snake? (15)   four Beautiful Firetails? (21)   two Eastern Barred Bandicoots? (13)   Spotted Grass Frog?

Tasmanian Masked Owl? (22)

two Tasmanian Hairy Cicadas? (28)

Dusky Antechinus? (14)

Wombat? (5)

two Green Rosellas? (19)

Can you find the

 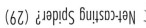

"The Bush Olympics," said the sign,
"Enter now while there's still time!"
Kokey Koala thought for a minute,
"Yes, I can do it, I must be in it."

Kokey knew if he wanted to win
There'd be no more lazing or sleeping in.
Each day he had to train, train, train,
In heat and cold, or even rain.

oral Emblem of New South Wales? (41)

BUSH OLYMPICS

To SYDNEY

Marlene Nash.

Can you find the

Female Bowerbird? (23)

Lace Monitor? (1)

two Spotted-tailed Quolls? (20)

Kookaburra? (14)

Wasps and nest? (32)

Blue-winged Parrot? (23)

Monitor Lizard? (14)

two Sugar Gliders? (7)

two Long-nosed Bandicoots? (3)

Can you find the · Tiger Snake? (13)

The big day came, it was bright and clear,
Around they marched, all full of cheer.
"Kokey, you can hold the flag."
His chest swelled up, he would not sag.

Can you find the

Mistletoe Bird and chicks? (18)

Spotted-tailed Quoll? (1)

Little Red Flying-fox? (9)

two Musk Lorikeets? (24)

Barking Owl? (21)

dwing Butterfly? (10) Floral Emblem of Queensland? (28)

QUEENSLAND RAINFOREST—Diving

To Brisbane

The diving was his first event,
A triple somersault—he bent,
Then jumped and rolled and rolled, OH GOSH!
He landed with an awful SPLOSH.

Marlene Nash

FINISH

If there was any chance of winning
He thought he'd do it in the swimming.
How wrong he was, he hooked the rope
And really did feel such a dope.

Claire Yerbury

vamp Hen? (25) Catfish? (10) Eastern Horseshoe-bat? (6) **NEW SOUTH WALES—Swimming**

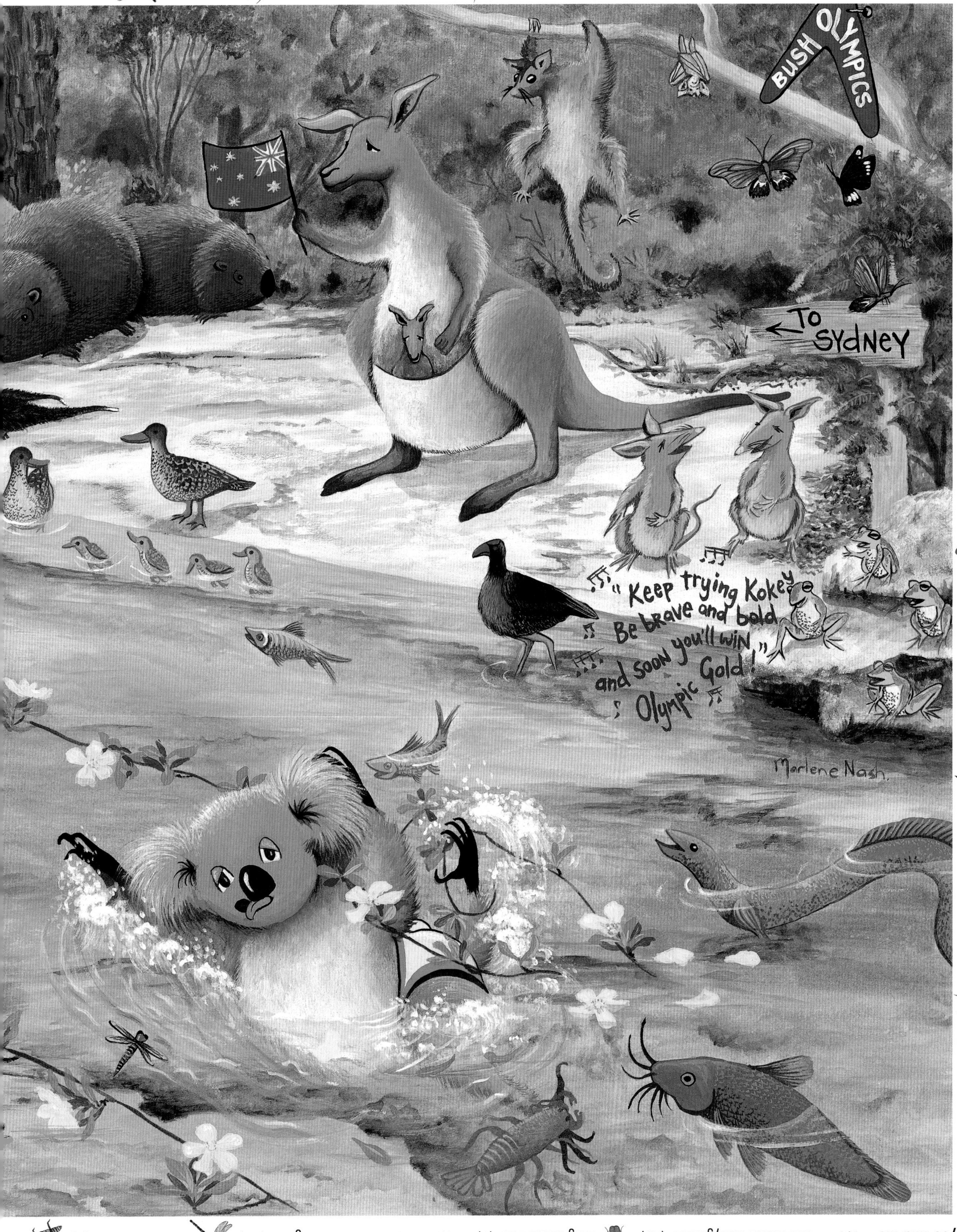

BUSH OLYMPICS
TO SYDNEY
"Keep trying Kokey
Be brave and bold
and soon you'll win
Olympic Gold!"
Marlene Nash.

Can you find the Black Prince Cicada? (27) Pelican? (20) Eastern Grey Kangaroo? (5) Brushtail Possum? (4) four Herrings? (11)

Can you find the two Brown Gerrygones? (23) Long-finned Eel? (9) Eastern Water Dragon? (16) two Wombats? (2)

Phascogale? (6)

two Common Brushtail Possums and baby? (11)

Common Dunnart? (1)

Whistling Kite? (17)

four Echidnas? (4)

Can you find the

To Melbourne

  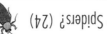

He found the hurdles rather trying,
He was so slow, he felt like dying.
He hit the hurdle, what a fright,
And ended up a dreadful sight.

Can you find the   Western Brown Snake? (18)   Western Quoll? (2)   White-tailed Black Cockatoo? (30)   Emu? (19)

Reticulated Velvet Gecko? (16)

two Honey Possums? (9)

five Cicadas? (25)

Western Brush Wallaby? (14)

two Huntsman Spiders? (28)

Can you find the

To Perth

FINISH

two Regent Parrots? (20)   two Ringnecks? (21)   Burrowing Bettong? (10)   **Answers page 29**

BUSH OLYMPICS

"Keep trying Kokey
Be brave and bold
and Soon you'll win
Olympic Gold!"

Marlene Nash

In the relay he would show his worth,
The other team had come from Perth.
He took the baton, ran like mad,
Then tripped and fell, he looked so sad.

biru? (14) Floral Emblem of the Northern Territory? (40)

NORTHERN TERRITORY—Canoeing

FINISH

The canoeing was another story,
He thought at last he'd found his glory.
But up from the bottom rose a snake,
He screamed, the canoe tipped into the lake.

Can you find the Northern Double Drummer? (24) Gould's Wattled Bat? (10) Barramundi? (22) Merten's Water Monitor? (30) Taipan? (28)

Can you find the Lotus Bird? (16) Spectacled Hare-wallaby? (6) two Red-winged Parrots? (18) Sleepy Cod? (36)

Can you find the Royal Albatross? (11) Hermit Crab? (23) two Eastern Grey Kangaroos? (29) Seahorse? (25)

Can you find the two Southern Brown Bandicoots? (9) two Blue Swimmer Crabs? (22) Caspian Tern? (14) White-tailed Spider? (31) Blue-ringed Octopus? (28)

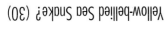 

Blue-ringed Octopus? (28) Yellow-bellied Sea Snake? (30) Grey Nurse Shark? (27) White-headed Petrel? (15)

Answers page 30

ck Cod? (20) Yellow Monday Cicada? (10) Osprey? (13)

NEW SOUTH WALES—Sailing

Can you find the Ringtail Possum? (1) two White-bellied Sea Eagles? (12) Leatherjacket? (21) Silver Gull? (16) three Dolphins? (26)

TO SYDNEY

The sailing should be more relaxing,
To stay on course it wasn't taxing.
The fog came down, he lost his way
And ended up outside the bay.

Can you find the

Children's Python? (18) Black-breasted Buzzard? (26) Beaded Gecko? (20) Bilby? (3)

**Now to the boxing he'd give it a try,
But halfway through he wondered why.**

three Red Kangaroos? (10) Brushtailed Bettong? (9) Praying Mantid? (16) Galah? (25) Pig-footed Bandicoot? (6)

He aimed his punch,
it missed and then,
He was down and out
for the count of TEN.

Alpine Oak Skink? (28)

Mountain Heath Dragon? (34)

Spotted-tailed Quoll? (5)

Broad-toothed Rat? (12)

Great Cormorant? (20)

Can you find the

 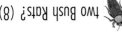

ombat? (11)  Floral Emblem of the Australian Capital Territory? (44)

SNOW COUNTRY—Gymnastics

BUSH OLYMPICS

The gymnastics was his last attempt,
To really know what winning meant.
He leapt and turned, one hand, now two,
At least he'd beat that kangaroo.

Can you find the

two Crescent Honeyeaters? (26)

Large Australian Raven? (17)

Metallic Cockroach? (36)

two Swamp Wallabies? (3)

Pipit? (25)

Can you find the

two Alpine Funnel-web Spiders? (27) Scarlet Robin? (23) Mountain Pigmy-possum? (6) Echidna? (2)

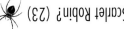

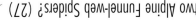

Can you find the 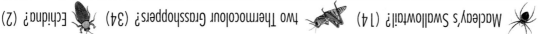 Hairy Cicada? (30)   Mountain Pigmy-possum? (6)   two Pacific Ducks and ducklings? (20)

Scarlet Robin? (22)

Ringtail Possum and baby? (7)

two Magpies? (18)

two Crimson Rosellas? (21)

two Corroboree Frogs? (32)

Can you find the

BUSH OLYMPICS

To SYDNEY

While on the bars he heard
the crowd roar,
TEN out of TEN, a perfect score.
So now he stood so proud and bold,

 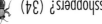

claire
YERBURY

ghlands Copperhead Snake? (28) Broad-toothed Rat? (12)

SNOW COUNTRY—Presentation

Can you find the

Swamp Wallaby? (3)

Dusky Antechinus? (10)

two Admiral Butterflies? (15)

Platypus? (13)

two Alpine Funnel-web Spiders? (26)

Three cheers, at last,
OLYMPIC GOLD!

Marlene Nash

Can you find the

Little Raven? (4)

two Olive Whistlers? (17)

Mountain Heath Dragon? (23)

Eastern Grey Kangaroo? (33)

Scene 1　Tasmania

(1) Little Pigmy-possum
(2) Tasmanian Devil
(3) Eastern Quoll
(4) two Echidnas
(5) Wombat
(6) Tasmanian Pademelon
(7) Gould's Long-eared Bat
(8) Long-nosed Potoroo
(9) two Tasmanian Bettongs and baby
(10) Brushtail Possum
(11) Ringtail Possum
(12) Sugar Glider
(13) two Eastern Barred Bandicoots
(14) Dusky Antechinus
(15) Copperhead Snake
(16) Oak Skink
(17) Spotted Grass Frog
(18) three Silvereyes
(19) two Green Rosellas
(20) Crescent Honeyeater
(21) four Beautiful Firetails
(22) Tasmanian Masked Owl
(23) four Painted Ladies
　　(males and females; the females
　　are paler)
(24) Ants
(25) Beehive and bees

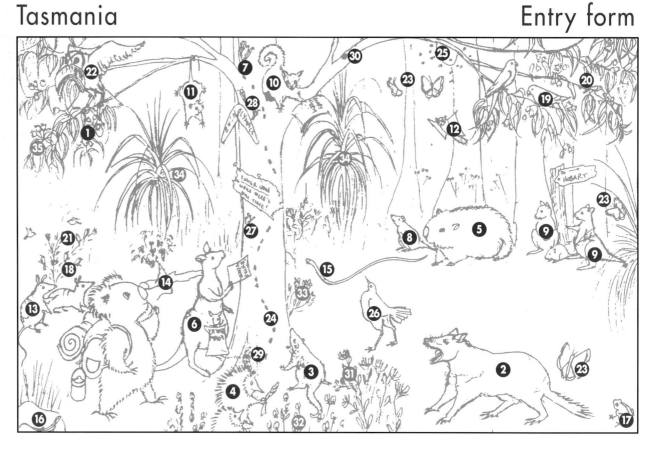

(26) Tasmanian Hen
(27) Tasmanian Tree Frog
(28) two Tasmanian Hairy Cicadas

(29) Net-casting Spider
(30) Bird-dung Spider
(31) Tasmanian Waratah

(32) Prickly Pea Bush
(33) Heath Milkwort
(34) two Pandanis

(35) Tasmanian Blue Gum, Floral
　　Emblem of Tasmania

Scene 2　Sydney, New South Wales

(1) Lace Monitor
(2) Phascogale
(3) Coucal
(4) King Parrot
(5) three Yellow-faced Honeyeaters
(6) two Echidnas
(7) Red-necked Wallaby
(8) Wombat
(9) Copper-tailed Skink
(10) Death Adder
(11) two Koalas
(12) Squirrel Glider
(13) Grey-headed Flying-fox
(14) Kookaburra
(15) Brushtailed Wallaby
(16) Ringtailed Possum
(17) White-cheeked Honeyeater
(18) Southern Bandicoot
(19) Lyrebird
(20) two Spotted-tailed Quolls
(21) two Blue-tongue Lizards
(22) Male Bowerbird
(23) Female Bowerbird
(24) Green and Gold Bell Frog
(25) three Blue Triangle Butterflies
(26) Yellow-bellied Glider
(27) four Rainbow Lorikeets
(28) Leaf-curling Spider

(29) Two-spined Spider
(30) Centipede
(31) two Green Grocer Cicadas
(32) Wasps and nest

(33) Grey Grevillea
(34) Flannel Flower
(35) Eggs and Bacon
(36) Rock Lily

(37) *Boronia serrulata*
(38) *Banksia serrata*
(39) Christmas Bells
(40) Wedge Pea

(41) Waratah, Floral Emblem of
　　New South Wales

Scene 3   New South Wales   Opening Ceremony

(1) Spotted-tailed Quoll
(2) Fan-tailed Dunnart
(3) two Long-nosed Bandicoots
(4) three baby Koalas
(5) Wombat
(6) Eastern Pigmy-possum
(7) two Sugar Gliders
(8) two Common Brushtail Possums and baby
(9) Little Red Flying-fox
(10) two Echidnas
(11) Emu
(12) Platypus
(13) Tiger Snake
(14) Monitor Lizard
(15) Tesselated Gecko
(16) Thick-tailed Gecko
(17) Eastern Banjo Frog
(18) Mistletoe Bird and chicks
(19) Yellow-tailed Black Cockatoo
(20) Kookaburra
(21) Barking Owl
(22) three Red-rumped Parrots
(23) Blue-winged Parrot
(24) two Musk Lorikeets
(25) two White-cheeked Rozellas
(26) Cherry-nose Cicada

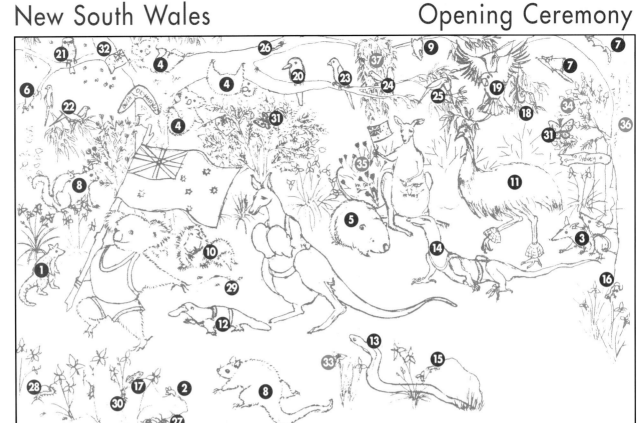

(27) two Redback Spiders
(28) Centipede
(29) Ants and nest
(30) two Grasshoppers
(31) two Swordgrass Brown Butterflies (male and female)
(32) Beehive and bees
(33) Flag Iris
(34) Bottlebrush
(35) Mountain Devil Bush
(36) Scribbly Gum
(37) Mistletoe

Scene 4   Queensland Rainforest   Diving

(1) two Antechinuses
(2) Platypus
(3) four Water-rats
(4) eight Rainbow Fish
(5) two Green Tree Frogs
(6) Paradise Kingfisher
(7) Golden Orb Spider
(8) Eastern Water Skink
(9) Ulysses Butterfly
(10) Birdwing Butterfly
(11) Hercules Moth Caterpillar
(12) two Black-striped Wallabies
(13) Red-legged Pademelon
(14) Tube-nosed Bat
(15) Striped Possum
(16) two Echidnas
(17) seven Tadpoles
(18) three Northern Brown Bandicoots
(19) Golden Bowerbird
(20) Daintree River Possum
(21) Dragonfly
(22) Diamond Python
(23) Water Strider
(24) Northern Snake-necked Turtle
(25) Blue Quandong Tree
(26) Water Lillies

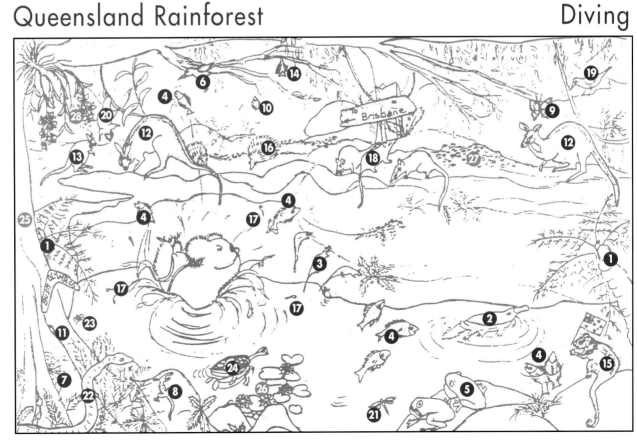

(27) Native Violets

(28) Cooktown Orchid, Floral Emblem of Queensland

Scene 5

(1) Echidna
(2) two Wombats
(3) two Water-rats
(4) Brushtail Possum
(5) Eastern Grey Kangaroo
(6) Eastern Horseshoe-bat
(7) two Long-nosed Bandicoots
(8) Platypus
(9) Long-finned Eel
(10) Catfish
(11) four Herrings
(12) two Mountain Galaxias
(13) Crayfish
(14) four Green and Golden Bell Frogs
(15) Red-bellied Black Snake
(16) Eastern Water Dragon
(17) Eastern Snake-necked Tortoise
(18) three Orchard Butterflies (male and females; females are paler)
(19) Darter
(20) Pelican
(21) two Grey Teal Ducks and four ducklings
(22) Kookaburra
(23) two Brown Gerrygones
(24) three Sulphur-crested Cockatoos

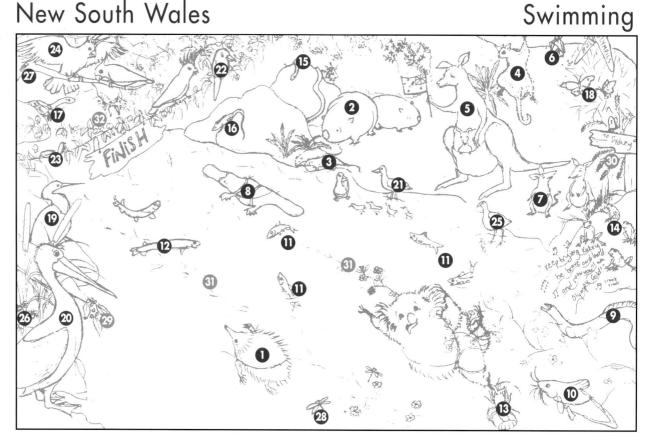

(25) Swamp Hen
(26) two Funnel-web Spiders
(27) Black Prince Cicada
(28) two Dragonflies
(29) Black Wattle
(30) Geebung
(31) *Hibbertia scandens*
(32) Native Wisteria

Scene 6

(1) Common Dunnart
(2) Lyrebird
(3) Long-nosed Bandicoot
(4) four Echidnas
(5) Agile Antechinus
(6) Phascogale
(7) two Eastern Grey Kangaroos
(8) Yellow-bellied Sheathtail-bat
(9) Spotted-tailed Quoll
(10) Mountain Brushtail Possum
(11) two Common Brushtail Possums and baby
(12) Kookaburra
(13) Tawny Frogmouth and nest
(14) Emu
(15) Sacred Kingfisher
(16) two Black-chinned Honeyeaters and nest
(17) Whistling Kite
(18) Powerful Owl
(19) three Wanderer Butterflies
(20) Blue Mountains Tree Frog
(21) Eastern Brown Snake
(22) White's Skink
(23) two Redeye Cicadas
(24) two Green Flower Spiders

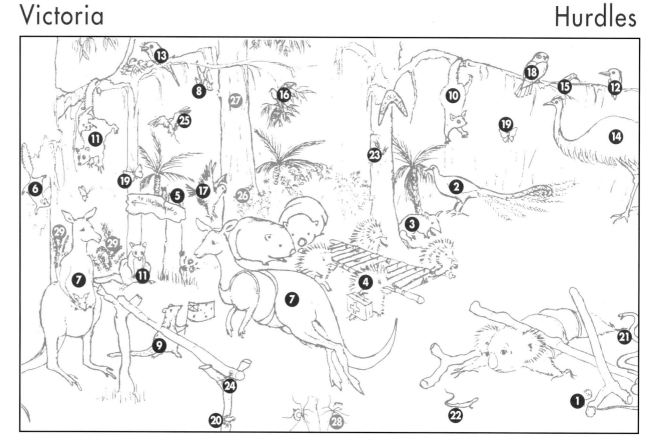

(25) Kestrel
(26) Dusty Daisy Bush
(27) Mountain Ash
(28) Spider Orchid
(29) Heath *(Epacris impressa)*, Floral Emblem of Victoria

Scene 7

Western Australia

Relay

(1) two Quokkas
(2) Western Quoll
(3) two Echidnas
(4) two Numbats
(5) Southern Dibbler
(6) White-tailed Dunnart
(7) two Western Barred Bandicoots
(8) Western Ringtail Possum and baby
(9) two Honey Possums
(10) Burrowing Bettong
(11) Rufous Hare Wallaby
(12) Tammar Wallaby
(13) Western Grey Kangaroo
(14) Western Brush Wallaby
(15) Western Scurrying Bat
(16) Reticulated Velvet Gecko
(17) Western Bearded Dragon
(18) Western Brown Snake
(19) Emu
(20) two Regent Parrots
(21) two Ringnecks
(22) two Rainbow Bee-eaters
(23) Tawny-crowned Honeyeater
(24) five Splendid Wrens
(25) five Cicadas
(26) three Meadow Argus Butterflies
(27) two Australian Painted Ladies
(male and female)

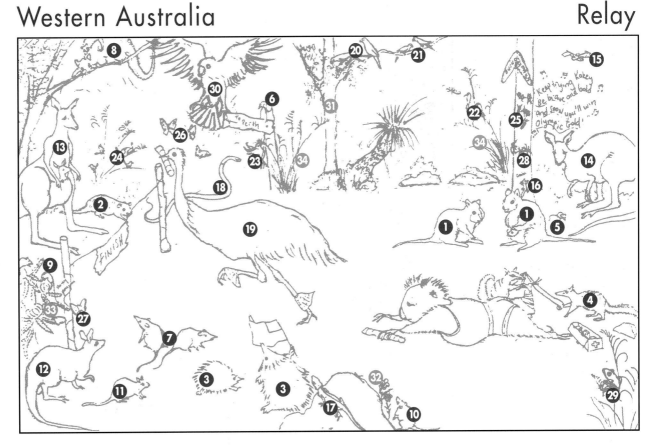

(28) two Huntsman Spiders
(29) Western Green and Golden Bell Frog
(30) White-tailed Black Cockatoo
(31) *Eucalyptus ficifolia*
(32) Leschenaultia
(33) Dryandra
(34) Red and Green Kangaroo Paw, Floral Emblem of Western Australia

Scene 8

Northern Territory

Canoeing

(1) two Echidnas
(2) Northern Quoll
(3) Kakadu Dunnart
(4) two Northern Bandicoots
(5) Rock Ringtail Possum
(6) Spectacled Hare-wallaby
(7) Agile Wallaby
(8) Antelopine Wallaby
(9) Black Wallaroo
(10) Gould's Wattled Bat
(11) Golden-backed Tree-rat
(12) Delicate Mouse
(13) Dingo
(14) Jabiru
(15) Plumed Whistling Duck and ducklings
(16) Lotus Bird
(17) Blue-winged Kookaburra
(18) two Red-winged Parrots
(19) two Star Finches
(20) two Crimson Finches
(21) two Gouldian Finches
(22) Barramundi
(23) Leichhardt's Grasshopper
(24) Northern Double Drummer
(25) three Blue-banded Egg-flies
(26) Freshwater Crocodile
(27) Common Tree Snake

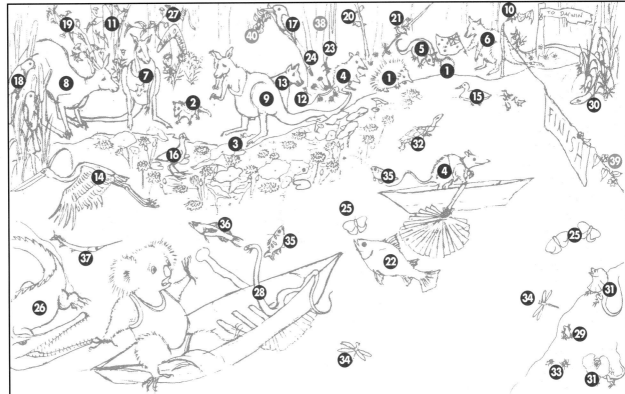

(28) Taipan
(29) Northern Dwarf Tree Frog
(30) Merten's Water Monitor
(31) two Frilled Lizards
(32) Northern Snake-necked Turtle
(33) two Jumping Spiders
(34) two Dragon Flies
(35) two Archer Fish
(36) Sleepy Cod
(37) Longtom
(38) Paperbarks
(39) Merremia Vine
(40) Sturt's Desert Rose, Floral Emblem of the Northern Territory

Scene 9   New South Wales   Sailing

(1) Ringtail Possum
(2) Wombat
(3) Yellow-bellied Glider
(4) Feather-tailed Glider
(5) two Common Brushtail Possums
(6) Grey-headed Flying-fox
(7) Large-footed Myotis
(8) two Echidnas
(9) two Southern Brown Bandicoots
(10) Yellow Monday Cicada
(11) Royal Albatross
(12) two White-bellied Sea Eagles
(13) Osprey
(14) Caspian Tern
(15) White-headed Petrel
(16) Silver Gull
(17) four Fairy Penguins
(18) Tailor
(19) three Red Fish
(20) Rock Cod
(21) Leatherjacket
(22) two Blue Swimmer Crabs
(23) Hermit Crab
(24) Rock Lobster
(25) Seahorse
(26) three Dolphins
(27) Grey Nurse Shark

(28) Blue-ringed Octopus
(29) two Eastern Grey Kangaroos
(30) Yellow-bellied Sea Snake

(31) White-tailed Spider
(32) *Banksia integrifolia*
(33) Flannel Flowers

Scene 10   South Australia   Boxing

(1) two Dingoes
(2) thirty Budgerigars
(3) Bilby
(4) Wongai Ningaui
(5) Striped-faced Dunnart
(6) Pig-footed Bandicoot (probably extinct)
(7) Desert Bandicoot (probably extinct)
(8) two Echidnas
(9) Brushtailed Bettong
(10) three Red Kangaroos
(11) Nailtail Wallaby (probably extinct)
(12) Common Wallaroo
(13) White-striped Bat
(14) three Common Dart Butterflies
(15) Thorny Devil
(16) Praying Mantid
(17) Military Dragon
(18) Children's Python
(19) Trilling Frog
(20) Beaded Gecko
(21) Bynoe's Gecko
(22) Gould's Goanna
(23) two Major Mitchell Cockatoos
(24) two Little Corellas
(25) Galah
(26) Black-breasted Buzzard

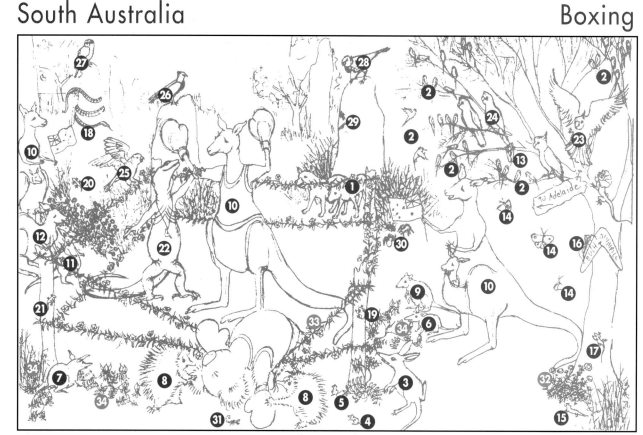

(27) Southern Bookbook Owl
(28) Spotted Harrier
(29) two Cicadas
(30) two Trapdoor Spiders

(31) Scorpion
(32) Poached-egg Daisies
(33) Blushing Bindweed
(34) Sturt's Desert Pea, Floral Emblem of South Australia

Scene 11

(1) Red-necked Wallaby
(2) Echidna
(3) two Swamp Wallabies
(4) Eastern Grey Kangaroo
(5) Spotted-tailed Quoll
(6) Mountain Pigmy-possum
(7) Ringtail Possum and baby
(8) two Bush Rats
(9) Agile Antechinus
(10) Dusky Antechinus
(11) Wombat
(12) Broad-toothed Rat
(13) Platypus
(14) Macleay's Swallowtail
(15) two Chequered-blue Butterflies
(16) Admiral Butterfly
(17) Large Australian Raven
(18) Little Raven
(19) Magpie
(20) Great Cormorant
(21) Pacific Duck
(22) four Crimson Rosellas
(23) Scarlet Robin
(24) two Olive Whistlers
(25) Pipit
(26) two Crescent Honeyeaters (male and female)
(27) two Alpine Funnel-web Spiders
(28) Alpine Oak Skink

Snow Country near Australian Capital Territory — Gymnastics

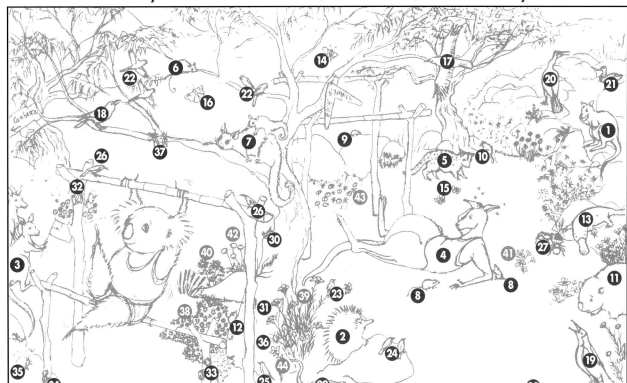

(29) Highlands Copperhead Snake
(30) Spotted Grasshopper
(31) Helena Moth Larva
(32) two Bogong Moths
(33) two Corroboree Frogs
(34) Mountain Heath Dragon
(35) two Thermocolour Grasshoppers
(36) Metallic Cockroach
(37) two Hairy Cicadas
(38) Silver Ewartia
(39) *Euphrasia collina*
(40) Silver Snow Daisy
(41) Caltha
(42) Scaly Buttons
(43) Carpet Heath
(44) Royal Bluebell, Floral Emblem of the Australian Capital Territory

Scene 12

(1) two Red-necked Wallabies
(2) Echidna
(3) Swamp Wallaby
(4) Eastern Grey Kangaroo
(5) Spotted-tailed Quoll
(6) Mountain Pigmy-possum
(7) Ringtail Possum and baby
(8) two Bush Rats
(9) Agile Antechinus
(10) Dusky Antechinus
(11) Wombat
(12) Broad-toothed Rat
(13) Platypus
(14) Macleay's Swallowtail
(15) two Admiral Butterflies
(16) Large Australian Raven
(17) Little Raven
(18) two Magpies
(19) two Great Cormorants
(20) two Pacific Ducks and ducklings
(21) two Crimson Rozellas
(22) Scarlet Robin
(23) two Olive Whistlers
(24) two Pipits
(25) two Crescent Honeyeaters (male and female)
(26) two Alpine Funnel-web Spiders
(27) Alpine Oak Skink

Snow Country near Australian Capital Territory — Presentation

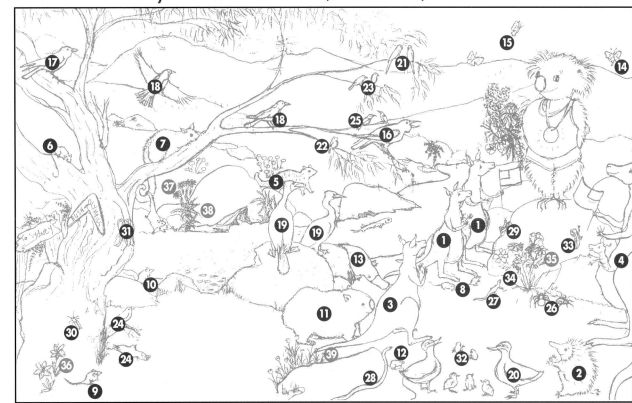

(28) Highlands Copperhead Snake
(29) Spotted Grasshopper
(30) Hairy Cicada
(31) four Bogong Moths
(32) two Corroboree Frogs
(33) Mountain Heath Dragon
(34) two Thermocolour Grasshoppers
(35) Anemone Buttercup
(36) Royal Bluebell
(37) Silver Snow Daisy
(38) Alpine Water Fern
(39) Button Everlastings

Bouquet: Floral Emblems of each State and Territory

My heartfelt thanks to my husband Paul for his patience, encouragement and trips
to the Post Office, to my daughter Elizabeth for all her helpful suggestions and
moral support, and to Jill and Leonie whose persistent nagging finally
persuaded me to put my poem and ideas into practice.

My thanks also to the Australian and South Australian Museums,
Universities of New South Wales and Tasmania whose experts answered
my many queries as I set about researching all the fauna and flora
for the book, and especially to Mary and Penny at the
St Ives Library from whom I borrowed many books.

Thank you also to Barbara in Victoria, and to Sue and Les
in Western Australia for taking photos of the bush in those States.

Finally, how can I thank my two artists, Claire and Marlene,
for their wonderful efforts? They have had to deal with a
very particular author, however I think the result
is now well worthwhile.

murray david publishing

Published by Murray David Publishing Pty Ltd
35 Borgnis Street, Davidson, New South Wales, Australia, 2085
First edition 1999
Reprinted June 2000
Reprinted September 2000
© Text Trixie Whitmore
© Illustrations Claire Yerbury and Marlene Nash
Airbrush by Ken Goldspink
Edited by Barbara Curran
Typography by Seymour Digital Art
Digital colour separation and film by Typescan, Adelaide
Printed in Singapore

ISBN 1 876411 34 1